If You Look Up to the Sky

Story by Angela Dalton   Pictures by Margarita Sikorskaia

For the strong women in my family tree
who are resting in peace in the sky
and watching over me.

— A.D.

In honor of grandmothers
who continue to weave the fabric of wisdom
through generations to come.

—M.S.

ISBN 13: 978-1-59298-828-0
Library of Congress Control Number: 2017906959
Printed in Canada
First Printing: 2018
21 20 19 18 17   5 4 3 2 1
Edited by Lily Coyle

Beaver's Pond Press
7108 Ohms Lane
Edina, MN 55439–2129
952-829-8818
www.beaverspondpress.com

When I was a little girl,

I used to sit on my grandmother's lap

and we would look up to the sky

and she would say...

If you look up to the sky
when you're feeling lost
and see the moon peeking
ever so slightly through the clouds...

know you're

in the place

you are meant to be.

If you look up to the sky

and there is no moon to fill it,

don't be afraid.

It is the sky

telling you to be

calm and patient.

Good things will happen soon.

If you look up to the sky and it is filled with stars,
name one after each of your accomplishments.

That way you're giving something back
to the universe that gave you
the breath to make them happen.

If you look up to the sky
and see a star streak across its darkness,
know that you are special and, like that star,
there will never be another you.

There will be times when you'll look up to the sky

and it will be filled with flashes of lightning and dark, gloomy clouds.

It is the universe reminding you

that even the bad times can be exciting,

and you just have to wait for them to pass.

And they will pass.

If you look up to the sky and see big, billowing clouds,

find as many shapes as you can.

It's the universe's way

of helping you create new dreams.

If you look up to the sky and it is a sea of blue...

the universe is telling you that anything is possible,
as long as you don't give up.

And while the sky is endless,

the years will go by.

Life will become busy

and you'll forget to look up.

But know that you will always find me
in the brightness of the full moon...

If you look up to the sky.